To Neysa,

SUNNY AND THE BORDER PATROL

COMPANION COLORING BOOK

MAUREEN YOUNG

ILLUSTRATIONS BY REBECCA POPOWICH

MYoung.

 FriesenPress

One Printers Way
Altona, MB R0G 0B0
Canada

www.friesenpress.com

Illustrated by Rebecca Popowich

ISBN
978-1-03-918439-8 (Hardcover)
978-1-03-918438-1 (Paperback)
978-1-03-918440-4 (eBook)

1. JUVENILE FICTION, ACTIVITY BOOKS, COLORING

Distributed to the trade by The Ingram Book Company

For My Eastsiders
Clark
Kasen
Kezia
Darson
Treyson

SUNNY

Tilting her head to one side, she sneered, "Step aside? Me? Don't think so."
(Chapter 1, page 2)

MARCUS ONE-EAR

"What do you call this?" asked Marcus, holding up a chicken bone with soggy skin hanging off it.
(Chapter 2, page 5)

ARTY AND HARROW

OR

"Small-ears! They just don't understand. We live here too," said Arty.
(Chapter 3, page 11)

WINTER STORES

"No, Harrow . . . you came in first," said Arty. "I came in eleventh."
(Chapter 4, page 16)

HAWKSEER

"Why would the Eastside Warren, send you two . . . if the warren is in such peril?" asked Hawkseer.
(Chapter 5, page 21)

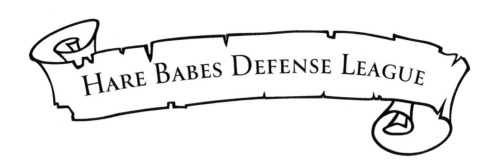

HARE BABES DEFENSE LEAGUE

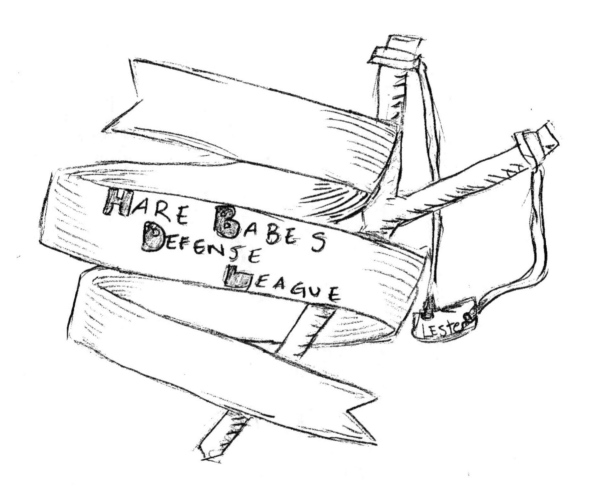

"I mean it, Mistress. No meeting during the captain's speech. We'll be good as gold," said Lester.
(Chapter 6, page 26)

WARRIOR GAMES

Captain Ruthers's voice rang out, "The games are about to begin."
(Chapter 7, page 30)

HEADQUARTERS

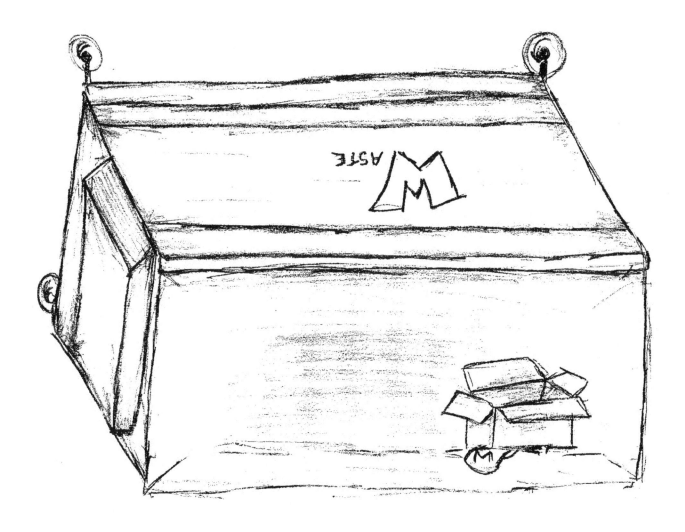

"Looks like we need more hares," laughed Marcus.
(Chapter 8, page 35)

DID YOU KNOW:

The most common rabbit in the city is not a rabbit? It's a hare…a White Tailed Jackrabbit Hare or Prairie Hare.

You can tell the difference between a hare and a rabbit easily. The hare will have long, black tipped ears, very strong hind legs and it will turn white in the winter. A rabbit, commonly a Cottontail will have smaller hind legs, shorter ears and do not turn white in winter.

Baby hares are called leverets. They are born with fur, open eyes and are ready to move around within hours of birth. Baby rabbits, known as kittens or bunnies are blind and naked at birth.

A group of hare or rabbit babies are called a fluffle.

Predators include hawks, owls, eagles, coyotes, bobcats, foxes, weasels.

Urban hares and rabbits have additional predators…dogs, vehicles and humans.

The Council

"Okay, I get that," said Harrow grumpily. "But I'm mad and plan to stay mad."
(Chapter 9, page 40)

HARE BABES

"Okay, you lot, listen up," said Lester. "I've decided to go on an adventure."
(Chapter 10, page 41)

LAUGHING MAGPIES

"I don't have cold feet!" said Arty, angrily. "I just know danger."
(Chapter 11, page 46)

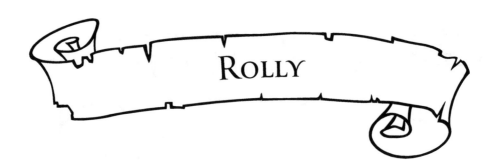

ROLLY

"My ma and pa threw me out. Didn't want a scrawny, no-good hare like me."
(Chapter 12, page 49)

LOW-FLYERS

"So many," said Arty. "I'd no idea."
(Chapter 13, page 52)

SEED CAKES

"Arty . . . Art . . . where are ya?" He looked back at the crossing and saw Arty, flat on the pavement.
"Arty!" yelled Harrow. "Get up!" (Chapter 14, page 57)

POPPY AND KNOB

"Well, I'll be boiled! Burrowing owls, if I'm not mistaken," said Lester.
(Chapter 15, page 60)

SHAWDOWFLIGHT

"I didn't know hares could swim," said the goose.
(Chapter 16, page 66)

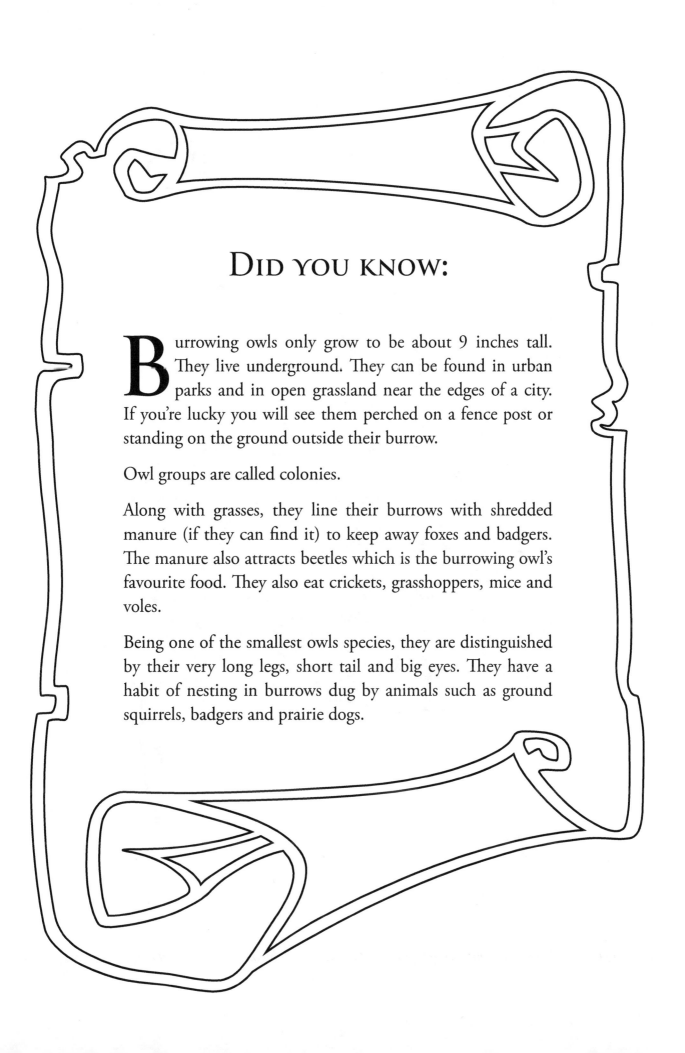

DID YOU KNOW:

Burrowing owls only grow to be about 9 inches tall. They live underground. They can be found in urban parks and in open grassland near the edges of a city. If you're lucky you will see them perched on a fence post or standing on the ground outside their burrow.

Owl groups are called colonies.

Along with grasses, they line their burrows with shredded manure (if they can find it) to keep away foxes and badgers. The manure also attracts beetles which is the burrowing owl's favourite food. They also eat crickets, grasshoppers, mice and voles.

Being one of the smallest owls species, they are distinguished by their very long legs, short tail and big eyes. They have a habit of nesting in burrows dug by animals such as ground squirrels, badgers and prairie dogs.

THE TRAP

"Flaming foxtails, Durg, look what we got here," said an incredibly big hare, as he tied the ends of the net together.
(Chapter 17, page 69)

ROLLY AND SUNNY

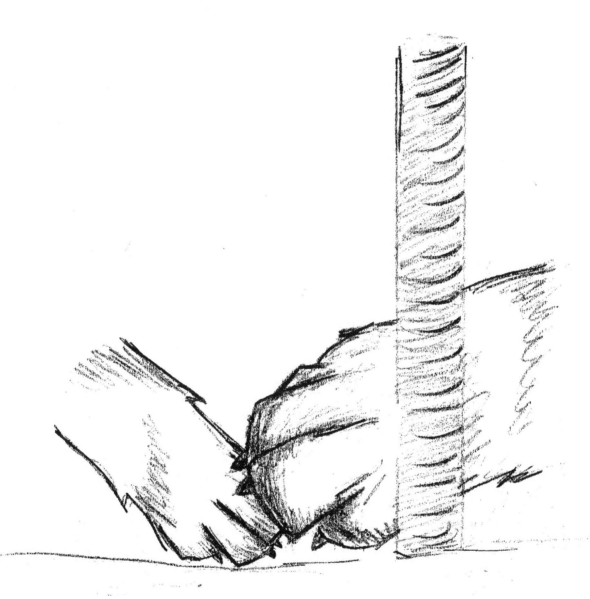

"We'll get out of this, Rolly. I'll take you home," said Sunny.
(Chapter 18, page 73)

CAPTURE

"Sunny, you were magnificent," said Arty.
(Chapter 19, page 79)

THE FEATHER

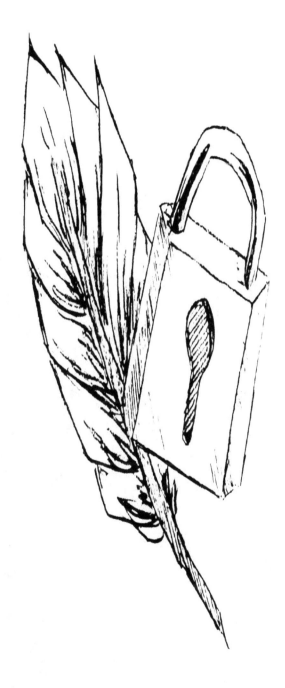

"Wow! Where'd you learn to do that?" asked Rolly.
(Chapter 20, page 83)

INNER CITY BATTLE

"What? Why you lousy, double-crossing, two-faced traitor!" said Marcus.
(Chapter 21, page 89)

LORD OF THE SKIES

"SQUACK," screeched the falcon, sending Lester flying back and landing on his rump.
(Chapter 22, page 97)

LESTER AND ROLLY

"Why, Rolly," smiled Lester. "The most delicious carrots in all the world."
(Chapter 23, page 100)

LUVERLY

"That's a beaver! A real-life beaver," whispered Lester. "He's enormous!"
(Chapter 24, page 105)

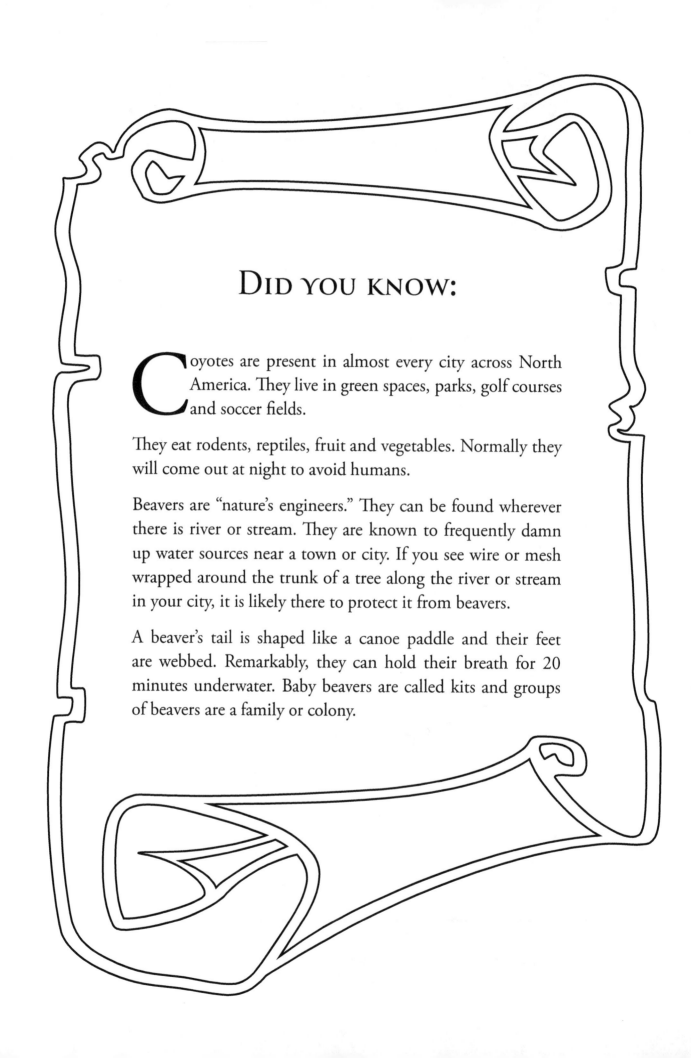

DID YOU KNOW:

Coyotes are present in almost every city across North America. They live in green spaces, parks, golf courses and soccer fields.

They eat rodents, reptiles, fruit and vegetables. Normally they will come out at night to avoid humans.

Beavers are "nature's engineers." They can be found wherever there is river or stream. They are known to frequently damn up water sources near a town or city. If you see wire or mesh wrapped around the trunk of a tree along the river or stream in your city, it is likely there to protect it from beavers.

A beaver's tail is shaped like a canoe paddle and their feet are webbed. Remarkably, they can hold their breath for 20 minutes underwater. Baby beavers are called kits and groups of beavers are a family or colony.

PREDATORS

Harrow whispered, "If there's just one, we might have a chance. If we run, we're done for."
(Chapter 25, page 109)

BEAVER DAM

"What would hares be wanting with this Big River Beaver Clan and Samuel Strongtooth?" asked the beaver.
(Chapter 26, page 115)

SAMUEL

"Luverly?" said Samuel. "But his name is Sage Strongtooth."
(Chapter 27, page 121)

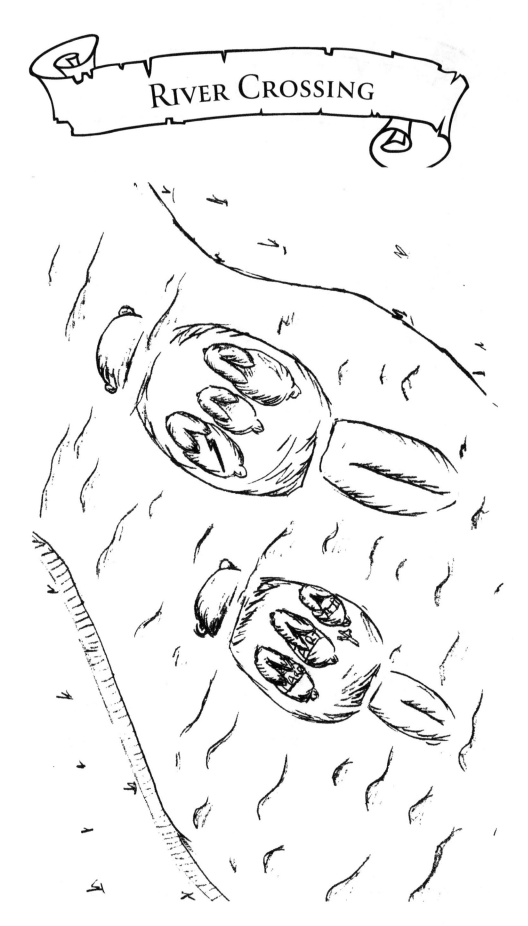

River Crossing

"Really?" said Arty. "We're to ride on Tubbs and Suze?"
(Chapter 28, page 127)

Harrow

"Sunny, see to Rolly," said Harrow. "I have a plan for this old villain.
(Chapter 29, page 133)

FRIENDS

"Wait a minute," said Sunny. "I had help."
(Chapter 30, page 137)

THE TUNNEL

"We're going to build a tunnel," said Suze.
(Chapter 31, page 140)

ARTY AND IMMERINE

"Come, Arty," said Hawkseer. "Now we begin."
(Chapter 32, page 145)

SUNNY

It's something I have to do," said Sunny
(Chapter 33, page 147)

Did you know:

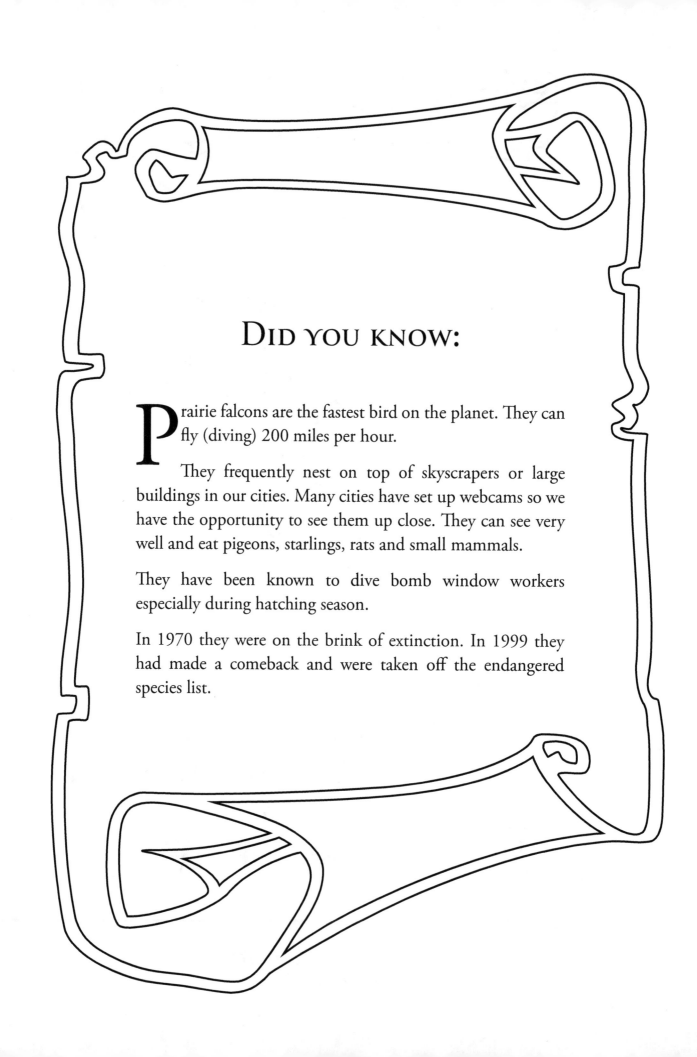

Prairie falcons are the fastest bird on the planet. They can fly (diving) 200 miles per hour.

They frequently nest on top of skyscrapers or large buildings in our cities. Many cities have set up webcams so we have the opportunity to see them up close. They can see very well and eat pigeons, starlings, rats and small mammals.

They have been known to dive bomb window workers especially during hatching season.

In 1970 they were on the brink of extinction. In 1999 they had made a comeback and were taken off the endangered species list.

BONUS PICTURE - MISTRESS MAGS

"Oh, how could I say no to such a smart-looking group? Okay, now gather around . . . just this once."
(Chapter 6, page 26)

Printed in the USA
CPSIA information can be obtained
at www.ICGtesting.com
LVHW051219221023
761808LV00007B/766